GROCOCO

A FRENCH CROW

by

MIREILLE & ARTUR

MAROKVIA

J.B. LIPPINCOTT COMPANY

Philadelphia • New York

GROCOCO

ONE NIGHT, during the Christmas holiday, snow fell on the French village where Ann and her friend Paul lived. By morning everything, from rabbit pen to château and church, was muffled in a white blanket.

The crows that lived in the church steeple peeped out and cawed gloomily. Some of them flew around a few times then went inside again. Their cawing was the only noise that was heard in the village that early morning.

Then the gray sky lighted up. Paul and Ann ran out of their warm houses with cries of delight. They both shoveled their way to the fence that separated their two gardens and there they met.

"I never saw so much snow in my life," Paul said. "Aren't we lucky?"

"Yes," Ann agreed, "we are lucky. But the birds are not."

"The birds!" exclaimed Paul. "Why don't they light on the ground instead of crying? They could feed under the apple tree."

"The apple tree," Ann asked, "which apple tree?"

"Grandfather and I, we keep one for the birds," Paul explained. "We never pick the fruit from that one. The apples fall in October, then the leaves fall and cover the apples, then the snow falls and covers the leaves. Apples keep nicely under a double blanket of leaves and snow, and birds love them."

The children shoveled a path to the apple tree. No bird was there yet. So, as they were tired of shoveling, they began to make a snowman.

They worked until lunchtime.

After lunch they came back. The sun had come out of the clouds, the snow was glistening, and black birds were at work under the tree.

"These are merls, you know," Paul said.

The merls were scratching in the snow and leaves with their feet, and picking at the apples. And they looked gay.

Ann and Paul hid behind the old stone well and watched. They did not dare to move. Their feet got cold and their noses got red. Suddenly another black bird, twice as big as the others, flew down and joined the birds under the tree. They all hurried to make room for him.

"A crow," Paul said, "a crow!"

"It brings luck," Ann said.

"Caw, caw," cried the big bird looking around.

6

The children kept quiet. The bird picked at the apples, swallowing chunks so fast Ann was afraid he was going to choke.

Then, as suddenly as he had come, he flew up into the cold blue air. He grew smaller and smaller. He reached his home, the church steeple, and disappeared through a narrow window.

"You know, it does not happen very often that a crow flies down from his church steeple into someone's garden," said Paul proudly.

"Crows are smart," Ann said. "This one will come again, now that he knows where the apples are."

"I am going to feed him every day," Paul said. "And I am going to call him Coco."

"Every bird is named Coco. Let's call him Grococo, he is so big," Ann suggested.

"Grococo is a fine name," Paul agreed. Then he said, "Let's finish the snowman; I have a plan."

They finished the snowman. And the next day, just before noon, Paul put a bowl filled with bread soaked in milk right on top of the snowman's head.

Grococo in no time discovered the bowl, and in no time emptied it. He did not mind a bit perching on a snowman's head.

When two days later a snowwoman appeared closer to the house, Grococo did not hesitate for one moment. With cries of delight he ate the food she was carrying.

By the end of the Christmas holiday the bird was perching on the head of a snowgirl who was standing right in front of the kitchen window. In her bowl, there were scraps of meat. Grococo looked so pleased that the children did not hide. They stood quietly and called him by name. And he answered, "Kiaw, kiaw." They liked his throaty voice.

9

Every day, even after school had started, Paul fed Grococo before he had his own lunch.

One day, however, he was late coming home. His parents were already seated at the dining-room table.

I will feed Grococo later, he thought as he was washing his hands at the kitchen sink.

Suddenly there was a knock at the window. Paul turned around. Grococo was outside the window. He was knocking and knocking with his strong black bill on the pane. Then he cried eagerly, "Krack-krack-krack-krack," and perched on the snowgirl's head.

"What a bird! I thought he was going to break the window because he had not got his lunch on time," Paul said to Ann later. Then he boasted, "Before long, you will see Grococo sitting at the kitchen table eating with me."

"And doing your homework." Ann laughed. "How lucky you are!"

"Some people have to go after a bird when they want one," Paul said. "But I...I just stay home."

But winter does not last forever. A warm wind began to blow. And the snowmen got smaller and smaller by the hour. Half a week later they did not look like snowmen at all. And everywhere brown patches of soft ground appeared among patches of snow.

Paul's pride was melting away with the snow. He kept putting food on the window sill. The food was eaten. But who ate it? Grococo never appeared. There were many small birds now, peeping merrily in trees and bushes.

Then it rained for nearly two weeks. When the rain stopped the black branches of the trees began to turn pink at the tip, and the brown ground turned green.

"Spring is coming," Ann said one day. "Get your marbles. We will go to play at Napoleon's square where it is fine and dry. All our friends are there already."

And they went to play with other children at their favorite playground. But even there the soil was still damp and the marbles got muddy. So when they reached home they washed them and lined them up on the window sill to dry. Some of them were made of glass. They shone like diamonds in the sun.

Just before supper, as Paul started to put his marbles away, he discovered that the beautiful shiny ones had disappeared. He looked everywhere but he could not find them.

A few days later, the children's mothers who had been sewing in the yard complained that their two silver thimbles were missing.

"Has anyone seen a magpie around here, or a crow?" asked Ann's mother.

Paul was delighted. "Imagine," he said to Ann, "Grococo is still around. He is playing tricks on us!"

They placed pieces of glass, old thimbles, and all Ann's doll's jewelry on window sills and around the garden.

But not one of the shiny things meant for Grococo was touched. Paul was disappointed.

"Don't worry," Ann said. "Grococo will come back when he is hungry."

"Yes, next winter," Paul sighed. "It is a long time to wait."

"Or if he is homeless..." Ann suggested.

This, of course, was impossible. The church steeple was a fine one. It was more than one hundred years old and it looked as if it would last forever. Grococo would always have a home, the home where his parents, his grandparents, and great-grandparents had been born.

Then, one hot June afternoon, the impossible happened.

The farmers were haying, and hoping they could get the hay in before the rain. The children were in school and feeling sleepy because it was so hot. The

crows were in the fields feeding. All of a sudden the sky turned as black as ink. Lightning flashed as never before. It struck the old church twice. All the slates of the roof fell off with an awful crash. Small beams caught fire. The big brass bells melted. Masses of brown horse-chestnut leaves tumbled down and were scattered around the church entrance. These had been the nests built by hundreds and hundreds of crows for years and years past.

In the evening of that terrible day Ann and Paul with Paul's grandfather went to look at the destruction. The old man was very sad. The children held his hands and thought of Grococo who was homeless now.

"Grandfather, do you think that crows have good memories?" asked Paul.

"Yes," the grandfather thought they did. "But," he added, "these are a special breed of crow, and a fine breed, too. They live only in church steeples or in very old ruins. And they won't settle anywhere else."

They looked up and they saw the homeless birds. They were circling and circling overhead and cawing in despair. Soon they flew away.

Paul was as sad as his grandfather.

But the next day Ann came running. She had seen crows sitting at the windows of the little clock tower that was on top of the girls' school.

"This gave me an idea," she said. "Let us build a big cage in the shape of a church tower."

And since this was a Thursday, their day off, the children started out at once for a nearby village where Ann's uncle had a little farm.

They followed a path through the fields. From far away they saw the nice church steeple of the uncle's village. They sighed and said nothing. They climbed to the loft of the farmhouse where there were all kinds of things that one could use to build a cage. There were also in the loft, and taking most of the space, big heaps of oats, wheat, and barley. The children walked around them very carefully for they knew that the different kinds of grain were used for planting and should not get mixed.

Suddenly, just as they were getting a roll of chicken wire out of a corner, they heard a mad screaming and cawing somewhere in the sky. They dropped everything. They ran and jumped, and climbed over oats and wheat, and onto the very top of a barley heap that was right under the window. From there they could watch a crow battle that was taking place around the church steeple. The crows that were outside were trying to get in, and the crows that were inside were trying to keep the others out.

19

And then a big black bird, just like Grococo, came to rest on the roof. He looked around. He cawed. He had Grococo's voice. Paul called him, and the bird cocked his head. At this very moment, the bellowing voice of the uncle was heard inside the house. The bird flew away. The children, their faces as red as poppies, slid down the barley heap. Then they saw the mess they had made. Not only were the different kinds of grain mixed but a good deal of it was pouring down the stairs. And...at the bottom of the stairs the uncle was waiting for them.

Luckily, right behind him the aunt came rushing. She announced that lunch was ready, and that, if it should get cold, she would not warm it up. When she saw the mess, she said, "Well, this is just what I need for my chickens."

And so the uncle calmed down.

But not so Ann and Paul. They could hardly swallow the good lunch. All they wanted was to go out and hunt for Grococo. When at last they were permitted to leave the table, the birds were gone and all was quiet around the church tower.

They went back to the attic feeling a bit depressed. But the uncle helped them find what they needed for their cage. And when they went home at dusk they had a cart full of fine building material.

They looked up at the church steeple far above their heads.

Where is Grococo? they both wondered. Maybe flying and flying, and not knowing where to go, maybe sleeping in the woods.

"It must be awful to be in the woods at night and to perch on a green slippery branch when one is used to a fine dry church beam," Ann said.

"And no bells," Paul said. "No music to put him to sleep or to wake him up."

"When he comes back," Ann promised, "I will play the violin for him."

"Ah, who knows," Paul sighed, "maybe he is in Chartres already, sitting on top of the most beautiful cathedral steeple in the world, and listening to the most beautiful bells..."

Ann did not like this idea at all. She was sure that Grococo would not go so far, and that soon he would be back.

But days passed and Grococo did not show up.

They started to work on the cage. Paul spent whole afternoons making wonderful plans on paper. But to build a real cage with wood and wire was another matter. He worked on it every day after school instead of playing. More than once he hammered on his fingers as if they were nails. Finally Paul got together something that indeed looked like a tower. But as he started to work on the roof, the whole thing fell apart. He was so discouraged he suggested they should wait until the summer vacation to begin building the cage.

Poor Ann was having her troubles, too. She woke up one morning with a toothache. Her mother decided to take her at once to a dentist in Chartres.

"Look for Grococo," Paul urged her.

She did not even answer. She felt wretched. During the whole trip on the train she kept holding her cheek. She did not see a thing.

At last the dentist was finished with her bad tooth and it did not hurt any more. She looked up from the dentist's chair. Just in front of her, through the window, she saw the high roofs of the houses and their chimney pots. She saw green trees and, towering far above houses and trees, two great steeples of stone so tall and pointed they seemed to pierce the sky. Around them, circling endlessly, she saw birds. They looked as small as flies.

The bells began to peal slowly, beautifully. At once Ann felt happy and strong.

"This little girl has been very brave," the dentist was saying, "she deserves a reward."

"Yes, yes," said her mother, "what would you like, my little Ann?"

Ann pointed at the steeples and cried, "I want to climb to the top!"

The dentist and the mother were amazed.

Thirty minutes later, Ann was climbing the winding stone stairs of one of the towers. The steps had not been made for the legs of a little girl; they were very high. But the guide, a big man wearing a navy blue uniform with gold buttons, said that she was doing very well. And all the tourists who were climbing behind nodded their heads and smiled.

"Are the birds much farther up?" Ann asked.

"The birds?" exclaimed the guide. "Is it what you are after? You will never climb that high, my child."

So Ann told him how the church steeple in her village had been destroyed. And how the crows had been forced to look for another home.

"I think the cathedral would be just fine for them," she said.

"Country birds will always be country birds," replied the guide. "They can fly to Orléans, to Reims, or even to Paris where there are big beautiful cathedrals, too. But they will always go back to their little village and their little church."

Ann had hoped to find Grococo in Chartres and bring him home. But now, she was feeling the tiredness in her legs and she was glad after all to hear that Grococo would go home by himself.

The guide handed her a telescope saying that she could use it without paying. Ann looked through the telescope. She saw a thousand niches topped by canopies of stone lace. And in the niches she saw many birds. They were resting there, among statues of saints and angels. They could listen to the music of bells and watch pink clouds drifting by.

"Just like in a big big fairy-tale palace in the sky," she told Paul afterwards.

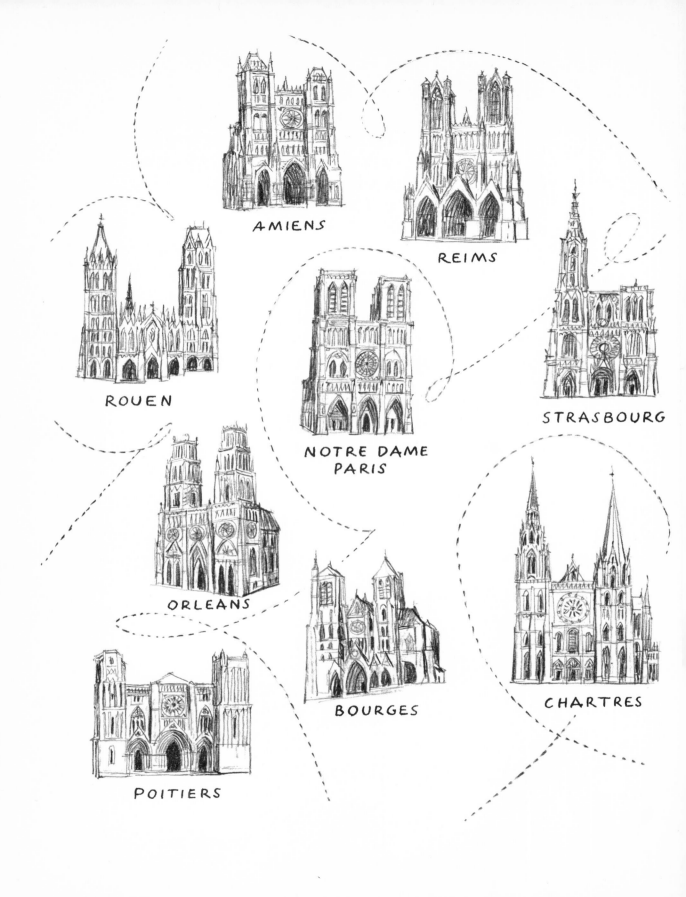

AMIENS

REIMS

ROUEN

NOTRE DAME
PARIS

STRASBOURG

ORLEANS

BOURGES

CHARTRES

POITIERS

But Paul was worried by the news. He brought out a map of France. He pointed at the hundreds of cities big and small. All of them had one, or two, or more churches. If Grococo visited only cathedrals which were the largest and the highest, he would still have the choice of forty-five cities.

"Grococo's trip around France is going to last forever," sighed Paul.

"He will be awfully tired when he comes home," Ann said, "and he will be glad to have a cage."

They asked Paul's grandfather for help. He said he would be glad to help them.

"But," he warned, "such a cage cannot be built in one day."

And since he could not tell how many days it would take, the children were worried. "Let's hope Grococo won't be back before his cage is ready," they kept saying.

Finally they decided that if he arrived about mid-August, it would be just right.

But the whole month of August passed, September came and went, and Grococo had not come.

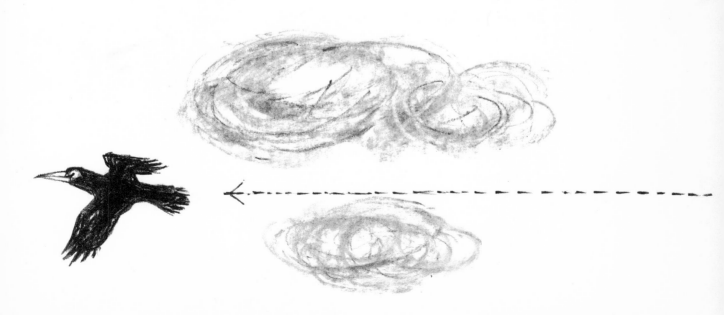

And soon it was October. Paul stood looking sadly at the cage under the apple tree. The apples were yellow, the leaves were red and brown and the cage was empty. My, my, Paul thought, if somebody had told me that Grococo would not be back before Ann's birthday, I would never have believed it. And tomorrow is Ann's birthday!

Then he remembered he had no present for her. He hurried to his room and began to search in a chest where he kept his most precious belongings. He found a case with a necklace that a traveling uncle had once sent him from Africa.

I never knew why my uncle sent that necklace to me, Paul thought. But it will make a fine present. He went to the kitchen window to have a look at the beads with the sun shining on them. Then he replaced the necklace in its case, put the open case between two pots of geraniums on the window sill. He went out in the yard and admired the display. Then he dashed through the garden toward Ann's house. Now that he had a present for her he could not wait to give it to her. But Ann had gone to the baker so Paul had to look for her in the village. When he at last found her he had almost no patience left.

"Come, come," he said, "you must see *it* before sundown."

Ann did not get a chance to ask a question. She ran, holding her bread under her arm.

They reached the garden gate, pushed it, slammed it, ran again... Suddenly Ann stopped Paul. "I thought I heard Grococo's voice," she whispered.

"Never mind Grococo," Paul said. "Walk around the corner, and open your eyes..."

"I see nothing special," Ann said.

The smile on Paul's face vanished.

And indeed, on the window sill, between two pots of geraniums, there was only an open case . . . empty.

Paul began to search all over the yard and in the kitchen. He was frantic. Finally he said, "Somebody stole it. Somebody stole Queen Ranavallo's necklace."

"Queen Ranavallo? Who is Queen Ranavallo?" Ann asked.

"Don't you know?" Paul cried. "Queen Ranavallo was the last queen of Madagascar. And Madagascar, as you must know, is a big big African island, bigger than France even. Here is a portrait of the Queen." And he showed Ann a fine portrait painted on the case.

"The necklace I wanted to give you was exactly like the one on the picture," Paul said.

"Was it really the queen's necklace?" Ann asked.

"It was exactly like the one on the picture," Paul repeated.

When she heard this Ann felt quite sad and a bit scared. She wanted to go to the gendarme at once.

Paul thought for a moment. Then he said, "If I tell the gendarme, he will tell Father, and Mother, and Grandfather. This is going to make a lot of trouble. I'd rather find the thief myself."

"I will help you," Ann promised.

They put the case away before Paul's parents came home.

Then they started on a detective job. But the footmarks around the house, the holes in the fence, the locks of the doors told them nothing. They asked sly questions of friends and neighbors, and even strangers. They got nowhere. After a few days Paul lost his appetite and had bad dreams. His mother said she heard him talking in his sleep about a black queen. Finally she kept him in bed and put him on a diet of soup.

Ann came to call with her mother. While the two ladies were whispering in the dining room, Ann said to Paul, "You know what? I am going to ask Madame Violette. She knows everything."

"A fortune teller, pooh," said Paul. "I don't believe in them. Besides she is a witch."

But Ann paid no attention. She got all the money out of her china pig. It was not an easy thing to do because the pig had only a very small slit to put pennies in, and it was supposed to sit on the mantelpiece in the dining room.

Then, even though she was scared to do it, she went to the house where the fortune teller lived. She had to walk quite a way out of the village. Then she followed a dirt road edged by old crooked trees and ditches overgrown with nettles and prickly wild shrubs. She climbed a hill. And there she saw a house perched on top of the hill, all alone. It had a big black old chimney with a squeaky weather cock on top of it.

Ann stood a long time before the garden gate. She could not decide to open it. She looked at Madame Violette who was sweeping dead leaves and burning them, and she said to herself, "My, my."

Suddenly Madame Violette turned around. She came swiftly and opened the gate.

"Bonjour, Madame," Ann cried, getting all red in the face. "I want to ask you something." And as she did not get any answer, she added, "I want to ask about Queen Ranavallo's necklace...It was stolen."

"Queen's necklace? Come in my child," said the fortune teller.

Ann, trembling a little, followed her across the garden and into the house.

It was dark inside. Ann could make out an enormous fireplace with a caldron hanging in it, a round table with a fringed cover on it, a chair, and, perched

on the chair's back, a big owl that luckily looked more stuffed than alive.

Madame Violette sat on the owl's chair.

"Sit down," she said, "and tell me your story."

Ann got mixed up telling about the mysterious disappearance of the necklace. But, all the fortune teller wanted to know was which day, and at what time of the day it had happened. And Ann could not tell because she did not know.

Madame Violette laid cards on the table, covered them with other cards, then turned them over. All the while she kept muttering to herself. Finally she said, "Here is *your* dark queen. And here is the ace of spades. And, as dark as the ace of spades is *your* thief . . ."

At that very moment there was a fluttering of wings right behind Ann's back and a big black bird flopped down on the table scattering all the cards.

Ann jumped up and ran to the farthest corner of the room. She saw the owl turn his head toward her and blink.

In a moment the old woman had grabbed the black bird. She tossed him onto the top of the grandfather's clock, and shook her long bony finger at him.

"You stay up there, do you hear me? I told you I will trim your wings if you don't behave," she said.

Then she turned toward Ann. "Don't be afraid, little girl. It is just a crow, and he is not very smart. He was sitting on my chimney on Friday the thirteenth. He wanted to keep house in my chimney I guess. Ah, ah, ah, not very smart that crow! I caught him in my attic the next morning. He was easy to catch. He is not shy at all."

But Ann was standing by the door clutching her purse.

"I want to go home," she said. "How much do I owe you?"

"All right, all right," said Madame Violette opening the door for her. "You owe me nothing. I don't take money from children." Then smiling as sweetly as she could, she added, "I will help you to find your necklace. Come to see me again."

Ann ran downhill through the fields, and straight to Paul's house.

"I found Grococo," she cried, "I found Grococo."

When she had told the whole story, Paul said, "I will kidnap Grococo."

But Ann did not like this. She made Paul promise he would do no kidnaping.

"Madame Violette was nice after all. And she will help us to find the necklace. It was stolen by a black thief you know," said Ann.

But Paul was now too excited about Grococo to care about a necklace. The next day he was up early. He went to school and by noontime he had worked out a fine plan that he explained to Ann.

At four o'clock, right after school, Paul went home, got his snack of bread and chocolate, and said to his mother, "I am going to play with Ann."

Ann went home, got her snack of bread and chocolate, and said to her mother, "I am going to play with Paul."

They met outside. They walked through back streets keeping close to the walls so that they would not attract attention.

By the time they reached the dirt road that led to the fortune teller's house, night was coming on. They could see lights at windows, and odd shapes of old trees and carts in farmyards.

"You could not see a black thief if there was one around," Ann whispered.

"Never mind the black thief," Paul said in a loud voice. "I don't believe that stuff anyway." And he kicked pebbles and began to whistle.

When they reached the foot of the hill Paul asked,
"Do you remember everything?"

"Yes," Ann answered.

They came to the garden gate. They were as noise-
less as cats. Ann stayed in front of the gate. It was
an old gate and it had no lock but Paul climbed over
the wall anyway. Then he tiptoed to the house and
stood motionless before the lighted window. The
shutters were still open. He could easily see through
the lace curtains. After a while he gave a sign and
Ann called in a voice as hollow as she could make it,
"Grococo, Grococo."

There was a commotion inside the house, and an angry shouting and cackling. Then Paul came running back. This time he dashed through the gate. He caught Ann by the hand and they ran downhill.

When they were safe in the village Paul said, "It is Grococo. I saw him. He flew down from the top of the grandfather's clock when he heard his name. And the witch grabbed him. And she trimmed one of his wings with her big scissors. I saw her. The witch, the miserable witch."

"I don't think Madame Violette is a witch," Ann said.

"She's not going to keep my bird," Paul cried, stamping his foot. "She's not, she's not!"

The following day he said he had a new plan. But Ann would not go along with him.

"It is not nice," she kept saying, "it is not nice, and I am scared."

"I want my bird," Paul cried, "I want my bird."

"Look," Ann replied, "Madame Violette does not know it is your bird."

"You told me she knows everything," Paul shouted.

Ann paid no attention. "Why don't you go and talk to her like a man? She will not eat you. Or should I go for you?" And as Paul did not answer, she added, "Or you could perhaps write a letter..."

"Write a letter," Paul said. "How do you write to a witch?"

And the whole day long, at school, he wondered about it. Finally he wrote his letter with the red ink that was always on the teacher's desk. It was quite a letter. It read:

> tomorrow morning at seven o'clock
> I will come to fetch MY crow
> I look like a little boy but
> don't make any mistake
>   I am PAPOOPOO the WIZARD

That same evening which was a Saturday, he went to Madame Violette's house all alone. He carefully tacked his letter on the door with four thumb tacks. And as he walked home in the dark, whistling and kicking pebbles, he was very happy and very proud of himself.

But he did not sleep well. He woke up a thousand times. At daybreak he crawled out of his warm bed. He dressed in the clothes his mother had put out for him the evening before. They were his Sunday clothes. He went out, walked through the empty streets, went up the hill all alone in the gray morning. His heart was beating loudly long before he reached the garden wall of the lonely house. He climbed slowly over the wall.

He saw right away that his letter was not on the door. He was sorry, because, to tell the truth, Paul did not really believe in witches. And he knew very well that Madame Violette would know he was not Wizard Papoopoo.

"What am I going to do?" he asked himself. "What am I going to do?"

Suddenly the shutters of a window flew open. He had just time to hide.

Now she will come, he thought.

But only a black cat came out of the attic through the cat hole, looked around, climbed down the ladder, went to the front door, scratched and mewed. The door opened enough for the cat to go inside, then closed again.

Then the chimney began to smoke, and there was a fine smell of coffee in the air. The boy shivered. He was hungry, he was sleepy. He rubbed his eyes thinking, Now, now, I am going to knock at the door.

Suddenly he jumped up. A black fluttering thing was tumbling down the high roof. Then it plunged into the hollyhocks that grew against the wall of the house.

"Grococo," Paul whispered as if he were dreaming.

And indeed it was Grococo. He was easy enough to catch, the poor bird. One of his wings was trimmed. And he was covered with soot from head to foot. But Paul did not hesitate one moment. He took off his Sunday coat, wrapped Grococo in it and ran home as fast as he could.

The first person he met was his grandfather. It was lucky because no one else in the house would have

been able to understand the situation, smuggle in the dirty coat, and prepare the right kind of breakfast for the worn-out crow.

When at last Grococo was safe in his cage, Paul fetched Ann. She was surprised and she was happy too. But she did not say much.

"I did not kidnap him," Paul assured her, "honestly, I did not."

Ann could see for herself that Grococo still had soot all over his feathers. No doubt he had made his escape through the chimney.

"But why just at the moment you were around?" Ann kept wondering.

"As I figure it," Paul said, "Madame Violette got my letter yesterday late at night. It made her so angry that she tried to trim Grococo's other wing. Maybe she tried to kill him. But Grococo escaped. And he went to hide in the fireplace. That was the best place you know. It was dark, and at night there was no fire in it. Then he must have spent the whole night climbing up that chimney. Look at his feet. They are still all dirty with soot although we tried to wipe them off, Grandfather and I. When she lighted the fire this morning Grococo jumped out thinking he was going to fly. Why, Ann, I saw him flapping madly with one wing in a big cloud of smoke... If I had been a little bit closer he would have jumped right into my arms."

Meanwhile Grococo was crouching in his cage. He did not look very happy Ann thought. And Paul explained that it was because his wing had been trimmed, and that it was a shame.

"But," Ann pointed out, "if his wing had not been trimmed, Grococo would not be here in your house."

42

Finally they carried the cage into the warm kitchen. Ann got her violin and played *Frère Jacques.* Paul sang heartily, "Ding ding dong, ding ding dong." And Grococo, probably remembering the church bells, cheered up. He shook himself, ate, drank, and began a careful study of his door.

43

For the next days Paul and Ann were so busy doing things for Grococo that they forgot everything else. And it was worth the trouble. Grococo was simply wonderful. In no time he learned how to open the door of his cage and soon he was hopping all over the kitchen, woodshed and yard. He knew he could not fly. And soon he also knew that plucking at his trimmed wing or screaming at it would not help. So he worked on his jumping, and he enjoyed it. He would jump up on the dog's back and go for a ride through the garden. Or he would wake the cat by tapping lightly on his head with his bill then quickly jump away and pretend he had nothing to do with such a joke.

Whenever he became tired, or sleepy, or bored, Grococo walked into his cage in a very dignified manner. He loved his cage. And no doubt he was happy at Paul's house.

As Ann said, they could all be happy if only they knew where the necklace was.

"I still think of the black thief every night," she whispered.

"I must say," Paul said thoughtfully, "this is the darkest mystery I ever heard of. And the worst of it is that I don't know what to do about it."

One Thursday morning, Ann went to Paul's house. Paul and Grococo were having breakfast together. The bird was dipping pieces of bread into his own bowl of chocolate milk. Then he waited quietly for the bread to get soft before swallowing it.

The children laughed.

"Chak-chaka-chaka-chak," cried Grococo.

"It means, 'What are you laughing about?'" Paul said.

Suddenly there was a mighty knock at the front door. Paul went to open it. There stood the chimney cleaner all black with soot, and smiling. It was the time of the year he made his rounds and cleaned all the chimneys in the village, so the children were not surprised to see him. But they were surprised when they saw the little white package he was holding in his big black hand, and when they heard him say, "Ah, Mademoiselle Ann, glad to see you. Madame Violette asked me to bring this to you, personally."

Ann jumped to her feet. She took the package and unwrapped it.

"The queen's necklace!" the two children cried.

"Ah, ah, ah," laughed the chimney cleaner. "Is this a queen's necklace? I found it stuck between two old bricks on top of Madame Violette's old chimney. Don't ask me how it got there. And don't ask me why Madame Violette wants to give it to you."

"Kia," screamed Grococo jumping up, "kia."

And he snatched the necklace. Then, holding it in his strong black bill, he hopped toward his cage.

"Look at that black thief..." said the chimney cleaner.

But Ann and Paul were looking at each other. Their eyes opened wider and wider. For one whole minute, or perhaps two, they could not say one single word. It took them that long to understand the biggest trick of all that Grococo had played on them.

"I wonder what is going to happen next," said Paul.